The Witch's Vacation

Story and pictures by NORMAN BRIDWELL

SCHOLASTIC BOOK SERVICES

NEW YORK · TORONTO · LONDON · AUCKLAND · SYDNEY · TOKYO

For Joseph

ISBN: 0-590-09839-X

Copyright © 1973 by Norman Bridwell. All rights reserved. Published by Scholastic Book Services, a division of Scholastic Magazines, Inc.

15 14 13 12 11 10 9 8 7 6 5   01/8

Printed in the U.S.A.

07

We know a witch! She lives next door.

My brother and I have so much fun with her,

we never like to go away from home.

But last summer we had to go to camp.

We felt bad because the witch
wasn't coming with us.

It was raining when we got to camp. They gave us a tent number, and we ran to find the tent.

When we saw the tent,
we were afraid to go inside.

What a surprise!

PIN BALL

SODA
COLA
ROOT BEER
GINGER ALE
GRAPE

CANDY

POP CORN

HOT FUDGE

We all put on our bathing suits,
but we couldn't go swimming.
It was raining even harder now.

Then I saw something funny.
In just one spot on the beach
it was NOT raining at all.
And someone was there waving at us.
Guess who it was.

The other kids thought our friend
was funny-looking.
One of them made fun of her bathing suit.

The witch just smiled and turned him into a terrific swimmer.

But just for a minute. Then she gave
all the kids some water wings to play with.

My brother built a sand castle, but a big kid
knocked it down. It didn't matter....

The witch helped my brother
build another sand castle.

We were so glad that our witch
was with us again.

The next day she packed a picnic basket.
But by the time we got to the picnic grounds
all the tables were taken.

So we ate on the witch's picnic tablecloth.

Then everyone hiked to Lookout Point.
The big kids left us far behind. The witch just
smiled. She said WE would get to the top first.

And we did.

The witch helped to make camping
fun for everyone.

One night the cook couldn't get the campfire
going. It looked as if we would not have
a weenie roast that night.

Our good old witch came to the rescue.

Having a witch at camp makes a big difference.
It was turning out to be a wonderful vacation.

Our witch was there the day I wanted
to go riding. There was just one horse left.
The kids called her "Old Nellie-Bones."

I called her "Nellie the Great."

And she was.

When we wanted to go sailing,
the witch found a sailboat —

— just the right size for us.

One day I took out a rowboat
so my brother could go fishing.
He wasn't having much luck, until —

the witch let him use her broom
for a fishing pole.

After a while, the witch went ashore
to take a nap.

We were having so much fun that we didn't see where we were going.

There was a waterfall ahead
and we couldn't stop.

We tried the witch's broom.
It only works for witches.

I wished for the witch as hard as I could.

Back at the camp the witch woke up.

She knew we were in trouble.

But she didn't have her broom.

How could she get to us in time?

In a wink, she changed the water to ice —

and rushed to save us.

Good old witch.

We flew back to camp.

The witch changed the ice back to water,
and we celebrated by having a swimming party.

It was the best vacation ever,
thanks to our witch.